Jack Breaks the Beanstalks

SUE NICHOLSON

Illustrated by FLAVIA SORRENTINO

Once Upon A Time...

...there was a misty blue mountain.

Quarto is the authority on a wide range of topics.

Quarto educates, entertains and enriches the lives of our readers—enthusiasts and lovers of hands-on living.

www.quartoknows.com

Author: Sue Nicholson
Illustrator: Flavia Sorrentino
Designer: Victoria Kimonidou
Editor: Emily Pither

First Published in 2019 by QED Publishing, an imprint of The Quarto Group.
The Old Brewery, 6 Blundell Street, London N7 9BH, United Kingdom.
T (0)20 7700 6700 F (0)20 7700 8066
www.QuartoKnows.com

A catalogue record for this book is available from the British Library.

ISBN 978-1-78603-567-7

Manufactured in Shenzhen, China HH092018

9 8 7 6 5 4 3 2 1

FSC
www.fsc.org

MIX
Paper from
responsible sources
FSC® C017606

Below the misty blue mountain
was a wild, dark forest and by the
wild, dark forest was a village.

The village had a stream and a duck pond and an old red apple tree
and it was home to Jack and his fairytale friends.

Jack loved climbing.

He was always climbing the pine tree near his friend Beauty's house...

...and the old red apple
tree in Griselda's garden.

'Now don't go climbing our beanstalks,' warned Jack's mum. It was spring, and their seedlings were starting to grow.

'The stalks will break and we'll have **no beans** to make bean stew for the village Autumn festival.'

'I won't, Mum,' Jack promised.

But that summer the
beanstalks grew taller...

... and taller...

... and **taller**, until
they were higher
than Jack's house!

Jack **longed**
to climb them.

'I wonder how far you can see from the top!' he said to Cinderella as they were walking home from school.

One night Jack couldn't resist any longer. He crept out of the house and started to climb the nearest beanstalk.

Creak!

Creak!
swayed the stalk, as Jack climbed through the leaves.

Then,
Snap!

The stalk broke and Jack tumbled down!

But Jack couldn't resist trying again –
surely he'd reach the top next time!
So he started to climb the
next beanstalk...

Snap!

...then the next...

Snap!

...then the next...

Snap!

...until all the beanstalks were broken.

Jack went to bed feeling awful.
What was he going to tell his mum?

'Something terrible has happened to our beanstalks!' cried Jack's mum the following morning. 'Did you climb them, Jack?'

'No,' lied Jack.

'Tell me the truth, Jack. Was it you?'

'No,' lied Jack again.

'Remember, *I*'ve always taught you to be honest,'
said Jack's mum. 'Did you break the beanstalks, Jack?'

'No,' lied Jack for a third time.
'It must have been Griselda's cat, Puss.'

Jack ran away and hid
in Griselda's apple tree.

'Whatever are you doing
up there?' called Griselda.

'I've lied to my mum. I told her that Puss
broke our beanstalks but it was me.'

'Oh dear,' said Griselda. 'Don't you
think you should tell her the truth?'

Jack nodded. He knew it was the right thing to do.

'But *I* don't know what to do
about our beanstalks,' said Jack.
'We have **no beans** now
to make **bean stew!**'

Griselda gave Jack a big purple bean.
'Try planting this.'

'It was me, Mum,' said Jack when he got home.
'I'm sorry I broke the beanstalks and I'm sorry I lied.'

'Oh, Jack, I knew it was you,'
replied his mum. 'I've been
hoping and waiting for you
to tell me the truth!'

'Are you cross?' asked Jack.

'Not now you're being honest,' said his mum, giving him a hug.

'Look what Griselda gave me,' Jack said,
showing his mum the bean.

Jack and his mum planted Griselda's
purple bean in the garden that night.

The next day they
had a **big** surprise.

The bean had grown like **magic** into a huge, leafy beanstalk
with a thick, strong stem that reached all the way to the clouds.

'Just look at those lovely beans!'
said Jack's mum.

'How are we going to pick
them?' asked Jack.

'I think you're going to have to **climb
the beanstalk!**' laughed his mum.

So Jack got to climb to the
top of a beanstalk after all...

FRESH BEAN STEW!

HONESTY BOX

...and he picked so many beans, he and his mum were able to make **lots** of lovely **bean stew** for that year's Autumn festival.

Next Steps

Discussion points

Discuss with the children what the word 'honesty' means. Talk about the importance of why it is best to tell the truth. Below are suggestions for discussion points about the story. These will help the children with their comprehension skills, as well as developing their understanding of honesty.

- Do you think that Jack was honest in the story?
- How did Jack feel when he lied to his mum?
  - Why do you think that people sometimes tell lies?
- How do you think Jack felt when he told his mum the truth?
  - Why do you think it is important to tell the truth?
  - Did you like Jack better once he had told the truth?
- Think about the ending of the story. How was Griselda helpful? Was it happy for everyone?
  - Have you seen or read other stories about Jack and the Beanstalk?
  - How is this story different?

Letter writing

Give each child some coloured pencils and a lined sheet of paper with a 2cm border. Ask the children to draw a beanstalk in the border and stick on bean shapes, cut from purple and brown paper. Tell the children to pretend they are Jack writing a letter to his mum saying sorry for breaking the beanstalks and lying. Before they begin, remind the children of some of the facts in the story that they might want to include. For example:

Jack loved climbing and as the beanstalks grew, he really wanted to climb them.
Jack felt terrible and was worried about telling his mum.
Jack told the truth in the end.

Allow the children to read out their letters. The letters could be displayed to remind the children about the importance of telling the truth.